Jessica

Christine Leo

illustrated by Kim Harley

MACMILLAN
CARIBBEAN

In a magnificent palace, deep in the clear, blue waters of the Caribbean Sea, Jessica lives with her grandfather.

Jessica loves being out and about with her friends, playing and swimming and riding the waves.

Best of all, she loves her grandfather's stories about the time when he was young. A time when the ocean was peaceful and clean. A time when the only litter to be found on the sea bed was the odd bit of treasure and remains of sunken, wooden ships.

'I'm an old man, Jessica,' her grandfather said. 'Would you help save the sea before it becomes polluted and spoiled?'

'I will,' said Jessica.

One day, when the sea was soft and gentle,
Jessica set off to explore. She headed north to colder seas.
She saw hundreds of ships. Some were like huge, floating cities.
Jessica had to swim away from the ships, to avoid the litter around them.

She'd travelled for many miles, when suddenly
she swam into something nasty.
Gasping for breath, she dashed to the surface.

Jessica had to fight through a thick, treacly gunge.
It was cascading in great globs from a huge oil tanker.

The smelly, dirty oil
was turning the sea
into a horrible shade of sludgy grey.
All around, sea creatures were in trouble.
Big, greasy trouble.

The ship was badly damaged.
Jessica was frightened, and could only think about getting away fast.

She sped off, her eyes half shut, searching for cleaner water.
She almost collided with a small ship.

With an enormous lurch,
she leapt into waiting, helping hands.

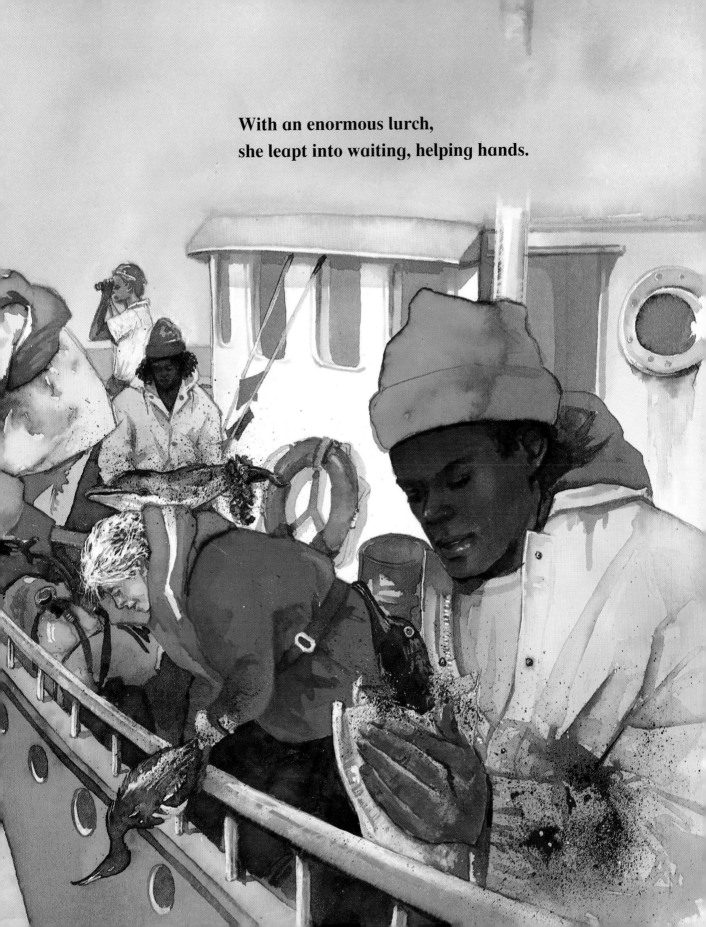

On board, there was furious activity.
'Who are you?' Jessica asked fascinated.

'We're the Green Patrol,' a young man explained.
'We're following the leaking oil tanker. It's a disaster!'

'I think it's sinking.' said Jessica.

'Yes, it is, but help is on the way,' said the young man.
'Our job is to save birds and fish that are in danger.'

Even though Jessica was tired and sticky,
she stayed and worked with the patrol.

Suddenly, she remembered that her grandfather
would be waiting at home, worried about her safety.

'Thank you for helping me,' she said to the Patrol.
She waved goodbye, leapt into the sea
and swam south. She was nearly home, when music came dancing
across the water. Jessica recognised one of the cruise liners
she had seen earlier.

There were thousands of passengers on board
and tons of rubbish polluting the sea.
She remembered her grandfather's words.

Jessica swam away and soon came to warmer waters.
A strange sound stopped her in her tracks.
Half hidden in the reeds, a male sea horse was giving birth
to thousands of babies. Jessica watched
as the brand new babies swam around on their own.
'They're beautiful,' she whispered.
'Aren't they!' agreed their proud father.
'But we are in great danger.' He told Jessica that hunters
caught sea horses to sell to tourists. 'They dry us out,
and bleach us, and wear us as pendants,' he said.

This made Jessica even more angry than she was at the polluters.
She decided there and then to join the Green Patrol.
'I will help the baby sea horses live in a safe, clean sea,'
she promised.

Jessica finally arrived
home exhausted
and fell into bed.
Her sleep was broken
by terrible nightmares.

She dreamt of the baby
sea horses being cruelly
hunted. She dreamt that
the sea had turned into
treacle.

She grew frightened for all
sea creatures. Even for the
enormous whales, the
smiling dolphins and
especially for the baby
sea horses, whose family
had lived in the sea for
thousands of years.

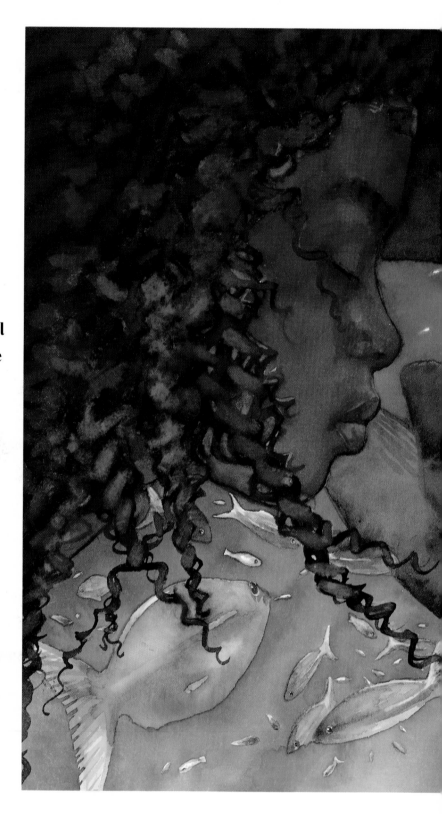

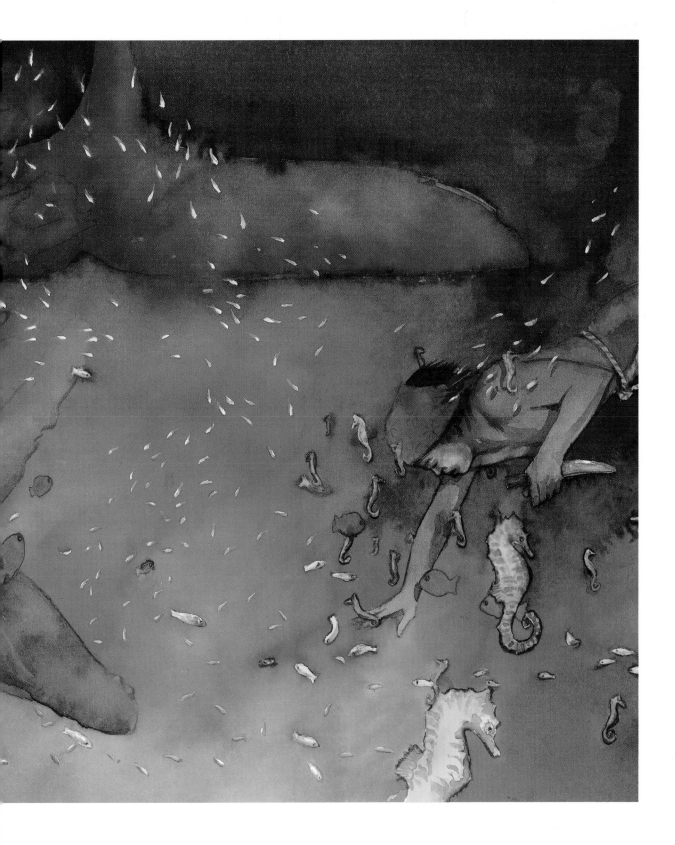

Early next morning, long before her friends called her out to ride the waves, Jessica contacted the Caribbean Headquarters of the Green Patrol. With their help, she set up a lookout post to scan the ocean. 'Can we help?' asked the dolphins.

'Of course you can,' Jessica said. 'Your own signals travel for miles. I feel much safer when you're around.'

A few days later, the dolphins bumped their noses against her window. It was their signal for her to listen. Jessica heard the steady thrum- thrumming of an engine. An evil looking boat was cruising around suspiciously.

Jessica set off to take a closer look while the dolphins stood guard. The boat was loaded with a dangerous cargo of poisonous waste. It was sailing around just a few miles from her home, waiting for a quiet moment, to secretly throw its horrible cargo into the sea.

Jessica quickly rallied her team.
The sea creatures helped her
weave a magic net.
Everyone had a special job to do.

The little sea horses
found pebbles with holes to thread around the edges.
These would hold the net down on the sea bed.

The larger fish and the dolphins spread the net far and wide.
The older sea horses and a few dolphins watched the ship
every inch of the way.

At sunset, just as the baby sea horses were being sent home to bed,
the dreadful sailors flung their deadly cargo overboard.
They were very pleased with their day's work,
and couldn't wait to sit down
to an enormous
meal.

As each poisonous barrel fell, it landed straight into the net.
'Heave Ho!' Jessica shouted. The net flew high above the evil boat
and opened wide. Drum after drum hit the deck.
The sailors leapt to their feet and scampered about,
slipping and sliding in the gunge that covered everything.

They were in trouble. Big, greasy trouble.

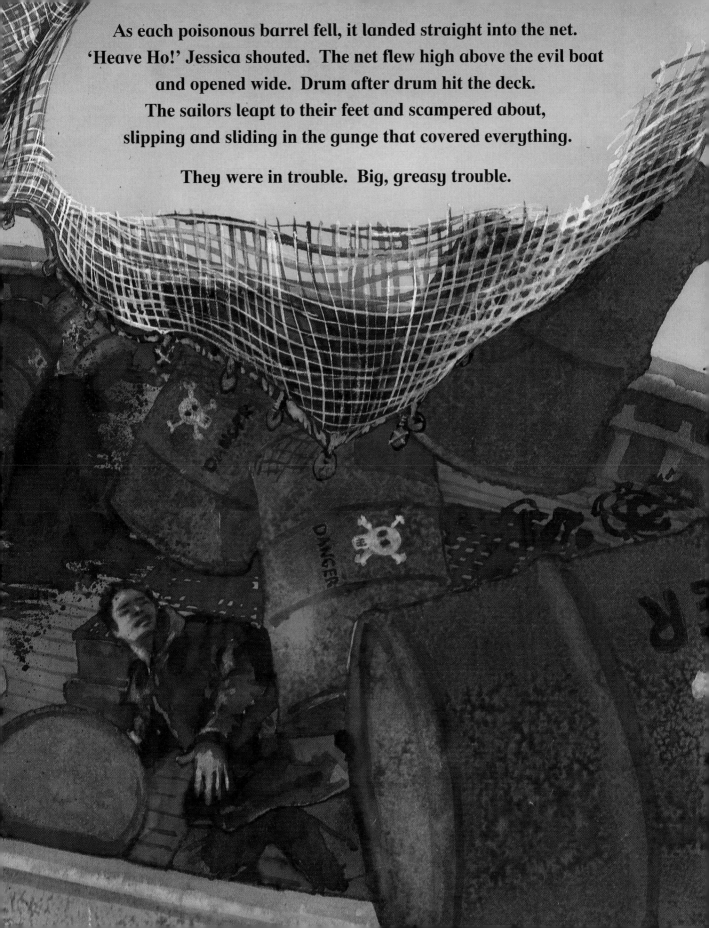

Jessica hurried home to send a message to the Green Patrol.
The Patrol chased the dreadful ship back to port where the men
and their evil bosses were punished.

She joined her grandfather
for an evening swim and told him of her adventures.
'Keep up the good work, Jessica,' he said with his huge smile.
'You know, my girl, this world of ours can be just wonderful.'

This edition of Jessica, first published in
the United Kingdom 1997, is published by arrangement with Tamarind Limited.

This edition published 1997 by
MACMILLAN EDUCATION LTD
London and Basingstoke
Companies and representatives throughout the world

ISBN 0-333-73456 4

10	9	8	7	6	5	4	3	2	1
06	05	04	03	02	01	00	99	98	97

This book is printed on paper suitable for recycling and
made from fully managed and sustained forest sources.

Designed and typeset by Judith Gordon
Originated by Reprospeed, UK

Printed in Singapore

A catalogue record for this book is available from the
British Library.